BILL'S
Christmas
LEGACY

SHAWN D. MOON
Illustrated by Jackie Brimhall

PRAISE FOR
BILL'S CHRISTMAS LEGACY

"A beautiful story about the gifts we don't often notice in our lives and how they truly help shape who we eventually become."

—STEPHEN R. COVEY
#1 *New York Times* bestselling author
The 7 Habits of Highly Effective People and *The Leader in Me*

"This story will lift you to a new level of faith and love. Shawn Moon has woven the deep questions of life into a beautiful message that moves and motivates us to remember the reality of life's tender mercies wrapped with Heavenly Father's love."

—RICHARD AND LINDA EYRE
#1 *New York Times* bestselling authors
Teaching Your Children Values

BILL'S *Christmas* LEGACY

SHAWN D. MOON
Illustrated by Jackie Brimhall

BONNEVILLE
BOOKS

AN IMPRINT OF CEDAR FORT, INC.
SPRINGVILLE, UTAH

ISBN 13: 978-1-4621-1089-6

Published by Bonneville Books, an imprint of Cedar Fort, Inc.
2373 W. 700 S., Springville, UT 84663
Distributed by Cedar Fort, Inc., www.cedarfort.com

LIBRARY OF CONGRESS CATALOGING-IN-PUBLICATION DATA
    Moon, Shawn D. (Shawn Daniel), 1967- author.
    Bill's Christmas legacy / Shawn D. Moon.
        pages cm
    Summary: As Mark prepares for his Mormon mission, he receives an assignment to provide service to an elderly gentleman who is severely limited in his ability to care for himself. The assignment is inconvenient and uncomfortable, but through his service, Mark gradually gains an appreciation for his neighbor.
    ISBN 978-1-4621-1089-6
    1. Mormon missionaries--Fiction. 2. Voluntarism--Religious aspects--Church of Jesus Christ of Latter-day Saints--Fiction. 3. Social service--Religious aspects--Church of Jesus Christ of Latter-day Saints--Fiction. 4. Older people--Care--Fiction. 5. Christmas stories. I. Title.

    PS3613.O5515B55 2012
    813'.6--dc23

                                    2012027105

Cover design by Erica Dixon
Cover design © 2012 by Lyle Mortimer
Edited and typeset by Whitney A. Lindsley

Printed in the United States of America

10 9 8 7 6 5 4 3 2 1

TO CAMERON, RYAN, MALLORY,
AND MATTHEW

FOR THAT WHICH YE DO SEND OUT
SHALL RETURN UNTO YOU AGAIN.

—ALMA 41:15

BASED ON A TRUE STORY

Acknowledgments

Special thanks to Ray Taylor, Thressa Knoell, Annie Oswald, Sam Bracken, Breck England, Bill Bennett, Zach and Hilary Cheney, Shannon Crawford, Tiffani Lindsay, Sam Hymas, Catherine Sagers, Mark Greenwood, Keith Leavitt, and Bill Shupe. Deepest appreciation to Harold Kay and Mayva Moon for their feedback and encouragement, and to Michele for her constant inspiration.

1

TESTIMONY

Eighteen-year-old Mark Tanner figured Bill Krause had always been old.

He'd once seen a photograph of Bill taken at his wedding, so there was at least some evidence he'd seen younger days, but as long as Mark had known him, he'd been old.

Mark lived just two houses north of "Old Bill," as he'd officially christened him, but saw him rarely. A stroke had assaulted his stamina, confining him to a wheelchair and to infrequent forays outside the walls of his modest brick home. Nonetheless, Old Bill managed to get to church every Sunday. That's where Mark interacted with his old neighbor most often.

The Krause family customarily gathered on a single pew toward the rear of the Third Ward chapel, with Bill's wheelchair positioned in the aisle at the end of the pew, a blanket always resting limply over his legs to protect him from chilling. His family would attend to his frequent needs—adjusting the blanket, wiping the drool, helping with the sacrament, or dealing with whatever occasional emergency might arise.

Mark remembered not one but many Sundays when, as a deacon, his position in the lineup put him at the Krause's bench. It was the deacons' responsibility, of course, to see that the sacrament trays made their way efficiently down each row, assuring that everyone had the chance to take the sacred emblems.

The Krauses' pew always aroused mild—and sometimes not-so-mild—trepidation. Mark would stand next to Old Bill but had to pass the tray across him and the wheelchair to Emmaline, Old Bill's wife, who always sat closest to her husband.

She must feel like a hostage to that wheelchair, Mark often reasoned.

The bread usually caused no concern, but the water (oh, the water!) triggered great anxiety. Mark always worried that Old Bill would bump the tray, spill its contents, and dampen the solemnity of the sacred ordinance.

If truth be told, Mark's real concern was more about how he might be embarrassed if he happened to be the one passing the tray that day. Though it never happened, it was always a risk.

Emmaline would take the tray and carefully place the tiny cup at Bill's lips and help him drink. The water always dribbled down his chin and onto his shirt. It happened every week; it was something Mark could count on.

The congregation could also count on Bill to share his testimony every Fast Sunday.

The testimony portion of the meeting was facilitated by a couple of members of the teachers quorum who carried two roving microphones and passed them around to those wanting to participate.

Instead of going to the pulpit as they do today, the participants simply stood and waited for the microphone to come to them.

Bill, of course, couldn't stand (nor could he speak), but that didn't deter him. He wouldn't wait for the microphone to reach him; he would just start yelling. Perhaps he knew that in his condition he would otherwise never get the chance, so he simply jumped in.

In full voice, he tried to express his conviction of the gospel and his gratitude for the ward members. His English was mostly incomprehensible, but his heavy German accent always asserted itself.

A small part of Mark admired Bill's tenacity and determination during this monthly ritual, but mostly he just made Mark, now a senior in high school, feel awkward. He had witnessed Bill's testimony repeatedly over the years; and though these episodes made him uncomfortable, other than on Sundays, he didn't give Old Bill or his family much thought.

The youngest of four children, Mark lived in a modest ranch-style home with his parents, Ray, a builder, and Sheila, a school librarian. He had two older brothers and an older sister, but his siblings, married or in college, all lived away from home.

The Tanner home, situated on the northeast corner of the block, included three bedrooms upstairs, an unfinished basement, and a fenced-in yard. Sheila had always wanted a finished basement, and occasionally she felt the irony of living with a master builder in an unfinished home. With two married children and the prospect of visiting grandchildren, she eventually persuaded her husband to finish a family room and additional bedrooms downstairs.

Mark, of course, was enlisted to help his father with the project. He'd toddled after his dad ever since he could walk, and as he grew, so did their relationship, which now was mature from years of working together to erect walls, lay floors, and install frames, windows, doors, and roofs. Under his father's patient tutelage, Mark had long engaged his nimble fingers in repairing household furniture and fashioning and repairing toys; he'd even built a dollhouse for his cousin one year. He handled tools with remarkable dexterity, and he needed no greater reward than to catch tags of conversation between his parents that revealed his father's pride in his development. Working with his dad left little free time after school, but he didn't mind, especially once his dad began paying him a fair wage as his assistant.

Their task now was a pleasant challenge. The basement's existing framing formed a basic skeleton around the foundation walls, but the individual rooms weren't yet framed in. There was one point at the base of the stairs where a studded wall had been erected, with a post centermost in the wall. The wall was load bearing, and the post supported the burden of the upstairs. It was a necessary part of the home's basic construction—if it were removed, the interior of the house would sag and ultimately collapse. But the current placement of the post didn't comply with the proposed room layout and would require careful repositioning.

The post consisted of three two-by-six boards nailed together then placed on a foundation board that ran the length of the floor. The top of the post was secured

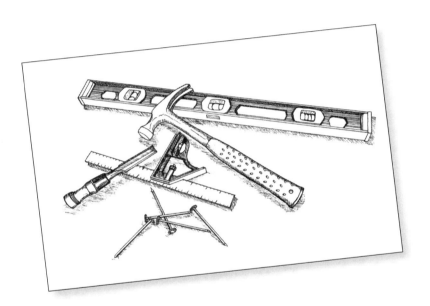

snugly against a beam that spanned the width of the home and ran parallel to the joists that formed the basement's ceiling.

Mark and his father carefully set temporary posts in place—two two-by-fours on each side of the existing post—before cutting the original post from its position. As they worked, the ceiling above them shifted ever so slightly before settling back in place against the temporary posts.

The week after Fast Sunday, as Mark and his dad were setting the new post in its permanent position, Mark asked, "What's a stroke, Dad?" He'd been thinking about Bill's most recent outburst and why the old man looked and acted the way he did.

"It's when the blood supply to the brain is disrupted," Ray answered. "Sometimes it's a rupture of an artery; sometimes it's a blockage, like a clot. The blood provides oxygen to the brain, and when it's cut off to a part of the brain, that part dies."

"Is that what happened to Brother Krause?" Mark continued.

"Yes," his father replied. "In Brother Krause's case, it's pretty severe. His mind seems clear enough, at least from what I can gather, but he's simply lost the ability to do some basic things for himself. He can't communicate well, can't walk, can't do very much without someone helping him."

"Can he ever recover?"

"In some cases, stroke victims regain some or all of the functions they lost. But in Bill's case, that's not going to happen."

"So he'll just stay that way until he dies, right?" Mark asked.

"Actually, he'll probably degenerate a bit as his body weakens," his dad replied.

Mark walked away from the conversation, shaking his head.

2

BILL

Wilhem Krause was born in 1911 in the tiny village of Neckartailfingen, Germany, a picturesque hamlet on the banks of the Neckar River. That scenic waterway originates in the Black Forest and meanders through the countryside for nearly 230 miles before emptying into the majestic Rhine River.

Many ancient castles adorn its banks, nestled amid rich green foliage, like massive monuments to the glory of Germany's rich history.

The village would have been a magnificent backdrop for adventure but for the harsh and lingering temper imposed upon the country by World War I. Money was scarce for Bill's family, food difficult to obtain, and formal education a near impossibility. Bill attended school only until his eleventh year, at which point he went to work for old Karl Kuenstler as a baker's apprentice. It was a heavy schedule that left little leisure time.

Every day, young Bill attended to Karl, anticipating his needs and learning his craft. This required a serious disposition, and his apprenticeship consumed nearly every waking moment. Karl was demanding and not always fair, but from this daily challenge, Bill developed a keen sense of responsibility and an admirable work ethic.

At eighteen, Bill immigrated to the United States, where he continued to work as a cook while he struggled to learn the English language. World War II broke out a few years later. As a new American citizen, Bill enlisted in the US Army. He loved his new country and had no reluctance to serve, but an inevitable conflict grew from the knowledge that both his brother and sister were serving in the German army. Bill would later learn of his brother's death at the Russian Front.

Bill joining the Church at an older age wasn't his own doing. He'd simply never heard of the Mormons, but when he met Emmaline at a dance on the army base one evening, he was instantly smitten by this tall, slender beauty and sufficiently motivated to investigate her faith.

He was baptized prior to their marriage (she wouldn't consider marrying anyone who couldn't attend the temple), and while his purpose for investigating and joining the Church was initiated by his attraction to his sweetheart, it led to a lifetime of devotion to gospel principles and quiet, simple service. Bill developed a firm testimony of the Restoration, a love for the temple (where he worked for many years), and abiding love for his Savior. He always struggled to master English, but he did understand with clarity two important things: the value of hard work and the importance of the gospel in his life.

After the war, Bill and Emmaline settled in an orchard-covered valley in north-central Utah, where they reared their five children. Bill found employment as a cook at the hospital, which he enjoyed so much that he frequently helped prepare dinner for his family following his shift at work. But he refused to bake—ever again. Karl Kuenstler had killed all his enthusiasm for baking. He could never boast of a luxurious salary, but the family's needs were met, and they never went without.

Just after his seventy-second birthday, Bill retired from his cook's position to work in his garden. A month later, he suffered his stroke.

3

THE ASSIGNMENT

*T*he assignment came in February, when the winter weather was lingering obstinately. For Mark, whose family had moved to Utah from Arizona seven years earlier, it seemed like the dregs of purgatory. The snow had been on the ground for several weeks, and its charm had long since faded. The sidewalks had been cleared, but persistent and trouble-some ice patches could occasionally upend an unwary walker.

On clear days, the sky was a stunning blue. The contrast of the crystal-blue sky with the stark-white snow was beauti-ful and, when juxtaposed with the rich, majestic texture of the mountains, created a postcard-worthy scene.

This scene, though picturesque, was offset by the biting cold. When the wind came, as it always seemed to do, the cold cut through Mark's layered winter cloth-ing like a surgeon's knife. Of course, he always had to take down the Christmas lights in this weather.

Sheila loved exterior Christmas lights on her home. Every year on the weekend following Thanksgiving, regardless of the weather, she would ask Mark to put up the well-used strand of oversized, colored bulbs on the soffit of their home. The years' relentless passage never seemed to wear down Mark's plaintive protest.

"Mom, why do we have to do this?" was his usual exasperated refrain, his eyes rolling to the back of their sockets. "Hardly anyone else in the neighborhood hangs lights anymore," he usually added. "It's stupid and embarrassing."

Nor did those many years of complaints from her teenage son alter Sheila's response: "Christmas lights are beautiful. Do it for me."

She recognized that her son's complaints had more to do with his resentment over this particular chore than they did the final outcome. Having successfully raised three previous teenagers, she understood that Mark's resistance would eventually pass and the job would get done.

After all, Mark loved Christmas as

much as the next kid—it was just the work he resisted. For all the care he took when he put the strand of lights away, it inevitably twisted itself into an insidious wire puzzle during its lengthy months of hibernation, surreptitiously biding time until the next Christmas. What's more, year after year, each bulb required testing, because if one light failed, the entire strand would fail.

The day of the light-hanging was always cold, sometimes snowing or raining and sometimes both, and the prospect of affixing individual lights on the roof seemed ridiculous. But as distasteful as it was to install them, removing the lights was even more unpleasant.

It usually took several reminders before Mark begrudgingly mounted the ladder and got to his task. He hated standing out in the cold—spring couldn't come fast enough!

Mark's father, Ray, came into his room early one Saturday morning shortly after the despised annual removal of the lights.

"Son, we just got a call from the bishop. We have a special new home teaching assignment."

Mark's smile faded. He admired his father's generosity, but he sometimes felt he overdid it. Like now. That "special new assignment" had a threatening ring to it. Unable to suppress a niggling agitation, and with something less than enthusiasm, Mark replied, "Oh. What is it?"

"You know Brother Krause. His health has been deteriorating lately, and his doctor is concerned. He's too sedentary, and this is going to lead to other problems."

"What does that mean?" Mark asked, sensing what was coming.

"It means he's not getting any exercise. He needs to get up and about to help strengthen his heart and promote circulation in his legs. His doctor feels this will help him, so the bishop asked if you and I would be willing to walk with Bill for just a few minutes every day. We'll need to support him—carry him to some extent—for a few hundred yards so he can move his legs and strengthen his muscles."

Mark immediately thought about Bill's regular outbursts in testimony meeting, and his annoyance was now completely transparent. "You mean we have to walk him . . . like a child? You've got to be kidding! Can't his family do it?"

"Mark, Bill is a tall, sturdy man. He needs to be supported by two adults just to get out of his chair. Sister Krause can't do it all by herself. And she is carrying heavy burdens with everything else she has to deal with every day. I know this seems like a tough assignment," his dad sympathized, "but you'll see—it won't be so bad. Bill Krause is a good and faithful man, and he needs our help. See you at four this afternoon." Ray gave his son an understanding wink and softly shut the door to his room, leaving Mark to sort out his frustrations alone.

"Four o'clock . . . every day! And in this weather . . ." the teenager muttered to himself. He'd always looked up to his father's testimony and willingness to serve others, but in this particular case . . . "What a joke!"

That afternoon, Mark buried his reluctance, bundled up against the winter, and accompanied his father to the Krause's home.

Sister Krause met the two of them at the front door. After greeting Mark with an enthusiastic smile, she gave his father a hug.

As Mark entered the home, he saw Bill sitting in his chair, bundled in a heavy wool coat, a well-used stocking cap pulled over his ears.

Mark's eyes were drawn to five gold-framed photos of the Krause children taken several years earlier and hung on the wall above a small upright piano. A worn floral-patterned couch covered in protective plastic, an armchair, and a nineteen-inch Zenith television with a rabbit-ears antenna completed the room. The home was tidy and sparse.

"Let's go for a walk, Bill," Ray said energetically, placing Bill's arm over his shoulder and carefully lifting him out of his chair.

Bill began to talk, but no one could understand him, so Mark did his best to ignore it. Bill smelled old, and Mark felt uncomfortable. Uncertain how to help, he reluctantly bent over Bill's form just long enough to take his other arm and place it over his own shoulder, as he'd seen his father do.

As they began to move toward the door, Bill slipped from Mark's shoulder, and Mark quickly repositioned and took Bill's hand in his to gain better balance. *Ugh*, he thought. *How did I get myself into this? This guy is heavier than I expected.*

It was obvious that despite his health struggles, Bill had lived a full, active life. His muscles had deteriorated, his body was weak and broken, but hard work had given him a solidity that still lingered. *Perhaps*, Mark thought, *this is why he's hanging on so long.*

The walk itself was mostly painless, but Mark was surprised at how long it took to go up and down one short stretch. He and his father, the two guardian protectors, took uncomfortably short steps, each holding tightly to Bill's hand with their outside hand, their inside arms wrapped tightly around Bill's waist.

The elderly man had some ability to move his legs, though not enough to support himself. His feet dragged sluggishly behind him like a reluctant dog on a leash, occasionally catching a step just long enough to temporarily relieve the weight on the two bulwarks.

"Bill, I've always been so impressed with your garden," Ray remarked as they walked, acting as if Bill were actually capable of a real conversation.

Internally, Mark rolled his eyes. His dad's acknowledgment of Bill's former service struck him as strange, given the monstrous daily inconvenience that was now heaped upon them. Nonetheless, as his eyes strayed to the snow-covered ground that had once been the neighborhood's miniature Garden of Eden, he had to admit Bill had been a fine gardener.

He owned the lot adjacent to his home, and back in his younger days he'd converted the entire piece into a giant vegetable garden. When he was still working, he'd awakened at 5:00 a.m. each morning to spend a couple of hours in his garden before his shift at the hospital kitchen began. After work, he'd scurried home for another companionable tryst with rows of veggies that inched daily toward maturity.

Weeds simply didn't have a chance with Bill, Mark remembered. He recalled the extensive field during planting time, covered with chunks of overturned earth,

each chunk a product of Bill's shovel. He'd had no modern implements to work his ground, neither tiller nor plow. By hand, he'd raked the ground smooth and readied it for planting.

"I used to watch you till the earth, going over the ground again and again to get it just right, soft and safe, and I wondered how you had the patience," Ray continued. "Yet every fall, you produced the most beautiful crops. We were always grateful for your generous sharing of those glorious vegetables."

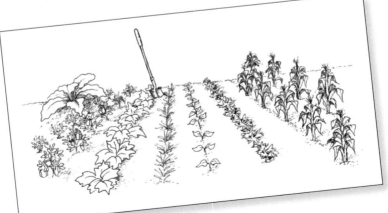

Silently, Mark conceded that Bill had been a generous neighbor, but this was small consolation as the days went by and the topic got old. Without fail, day after day, it was always the same: They would go on short walks, Ray would talk and-talk, the topic rarely varying—the garden today, the weather tomorrow. Bill would teeter and stumble between them with his weakened stride, which never showed any sign of improvement. Yet Ray would continue to talk without ever coaxing out a response—no improvement, no response, Bill's thoughts muted by disease.

Yet it was clear, somehow, that he was grateful for their assistance. Every day, as they carefully set him back in his wheelchair at the Krause home, Bill would take Mark's hand briefly and squeeze it ever so slightly. Occasionally, a solitary tear would wash down his cheek.

The walks didn't seem to change Bill's physical health, but it was plain to see he appreciated them. And as much as Mark protested the assignment, as he felt the first fruits of service, he too was impacted.

Winter eventually turned into spring, and with a few exceptions when the weather was most stubborn and inclement, the daily walks continued. Mark eventually began to feel more comfortable with Old Bill and even began contributing some to the conversation.

One day, as he and his dad were walking back to their home after their daily time with Bill, Mark asked, "Dad, I have a question. I don't mean to be disrespectful, but I'm struggling with something."

"What is it, son?"

"I hated this assignment when we first

got it. I resented the bishop, and, honestly, I was kind of mad at you."

Mark's father chuckled. "I know. You tried to hide your feelings, but it was pretty clear you weren't happy about it. To be honest, I probably wouldn't have been either when I was eighteen. But I knew you would feel differently after you had a chance to do it a few times. I'm proud of you for hanging in there with me, even when you didn't want to."

"It's not been too bad," Mark confessed. "At least not as bad as I expected. Sometimes I even look forward to it. But that leads to my question. I don't understand how a loving Heavenly Father would allow this man to suffer as long as he has. I mean, he can't do anything. He's basically helpless. He talks in complete gibberish, and he's been like this for a long time. What's the point?"

Mark's dad was thoughtful for a moment. "I know you're not trying to be disrespectful. Brother Krause has lived a long and good life. Wouldn't it be the merciful thing if our Heavenly Father simply called him home?"

"Exactly."

They walked together up their driveway and into the carport, neither one saying anything. As they approached the door to their house, Ray finally said, "Mark, I wish I had a good answer to this question. I don't. But here is what I do know: I know that we have a Heavenly Father who knows each of us. He knows all that we are going through—our happiness, our pain, our concerns, our joys, and our questions. He knows this for all of us, including you, me, and even Brother Krause. He is aware of all the pain and frustration associated with Bill's condition. Perhaps there are lessons Bill still needs to learn. Or perhaps his lessons are complete, but those around him still need to learn something. Again, that includes both of us."

Ray took the doorknob, then hesitated. Looking squarely at his son, he said, "Mark, you're eighteen. In a few months, you'll be nineteen and you'll have to make some important decisions. One of those will be to decide about a mission. I hope you're praying about this. It's a big decision . . . one that will change the course of your life. As you pray about it, perhaps you might take your question about Bill to the Lord. See what he has to say about it."

With that, Ray turned the knob and walked into the house.

Mark remained on the porch and thought about what his father had said.

4

MISSION

Mark followed his father's counsel and prayed about Bill's condition, but he didn't seem to get any insights.

"Dear Heavenly Father," he began, "we've been given this assignment to help Old Bill. He's a nice man, and he seems to appreciate our work with him. And

I suppose I'm grateful for the opportunity. But I don't understand why he's still around. He requires so much work, and I know both he and his family suffer because of it. Of course they love him, but wouldn't it be better for everyone, including Old Bill himself, if you could relieve him of his burdens?"

Mark remembered a seminary teacher's lesson on prayer. In order to receive answers, one had to listen. So after his question, he stayed on his knees and waited. Nothing came but silence, and Mark felt embarrassed for asking the question. He shrugged his shoulders. Some questions just didn't have answers; he was sure he wasn't the only person who felt that way.

"One more thing," Mark's prayer continued. "I'm almost nineteen. I have many things I'd like to do, and I'm not sure a mission is part of my plans. I intend to go, but I don't want to make the wrong choice. Is this the right thing to do?"

He prepared again to wait for an answer, but to his surprise, he didn't need to. Suddenly, he knew completely and clearly that a mission was the right thing to do.

The moment this realization came to him, Mark felt a swelling of emotion, an overwhelming sensation that filled him simultaneously with tears and elation.

While Mark's decision to embrace a mission was straightforward, it wasn't necessarily an easy one. After graduation, he'd become even more involved in his father's business, and he enjoyed the success that accompanies hard work, including a truck to drive and money in his pocket.

Nonetheless, when the call came to serve in Japan, he was resolved and ready to go. After eight weeks of intense language, scripture training, and far too much Missionary Training Center cafeteria food, Elder Mark Tanner found himself in the Far East, preaching the restored gospel to a wonderful but largely uninterested people. Mark loved Japan, loved the eccentricities of the Japanese culture, loved the food, and loved but struggled with the language. But even that came in time.

What was more elusive was success. Mark and his companions worked hard. They prayed frequently and fervently. They made their best efforts to be obedient to mission rules. Success was slow in coming (if success is measured by baptisms), but

Mark developed a deep appreciation for the uniqueness of this beautiful island country, the stunning vastness of Tokyo, the simplicity of the homes, and the goodness of the people. He grew to love the distinct seasons in Tokyo: the crispness of winter, the explosion of cherry blossoms in the spring, the verdant summer days, the blazing beauty of fall.

One day in late November, after Mark had been in Japan for nearly a year, he received a letter from his father. As he began to read, his eyes welled with tears.

"You will be sad to learn," his father wrote, "that our neighbor Bill Krause passed away last week. Our walks had become less and less frequent this past year, and they stopped entirely a few months ago. Since that time, his health continued to deteriorate. He eventually got to the point where he couldn't get out of bed. He finally slipped away one evening, surrounded by his family. We are grateful he is now at peace and released from the limiting conditions he struggled with."

Mark put the letter down, unable to read further. He'd been so busy with his missionary labors that he hadn't thought much about Old Bill these past several months, and he marveled at how emotional he felt. After all, he'd had nothing in common with Bill and he was nearly sixty years younger than him. He'd never even had a real two-way conversation with his elderly neighbor, in spite of helping steady him on their "walks" over the course of a few months.

Nonetheless, he recalled his last walk with Bill. By that point, Mark was talking almost as much as his father, and he was excited to share his enthusiasm about his upcoming mission. Old Bill's son had served a mission in Japan many years earlier, and Mark knew that as a convert himself, Bill held high regard for missionaries.

That evening, as he'd left the Krause home for the last time, Mark had lingered a few moments and then given Bill a quick hug. "Thank you," he'd whispered in the old man's ear.

Now Bill was gone. Mark agreed with his father—it was ultimately a blessing. But Mark would miss seeing him upon his return. Their time together had forged something meaningful in Mark's soul, and he felt the world was somehow diminished without Old Bill in it. For Mark, a mighty oak had fallen, and it left a void.

He wiped away his tears, then laughed softly to himself. "What an unlikely friendship," he said out loud.

5

CHRISTMAS

*D*ecember brought Mark's first Christmas in Japan. The weather was similar to home, but noticeably absent were lights, bells, tinsel, and trees. An occasional store displayed a picture of Santa, but for the most part, Christmas went unobserved in this largely non-Christian, Buddhist, and Shinto nation.

Christmas might be irrelevant to the Japanese, but it wasn't irrelevant to Elders Tanner and Bentley. These two youthful missionaries were determined to keep the holiday spirit as best they could. They cut a few pine boughs and propped them in a water pitcher in the corner of their tiny bedroom, then decorated them with a few paperclips and short lengths of colored string. They spread the few presents they'd received from home under their meager tree.

There would be few surprises, but they would still be excited to open their ties and shoe-shine kits on Christmas morning. (After all, what else does one send a missionary?) It wasn't the gifts that mattered, but the love that accompanied them. The constant prayers and ongoing support of their families were worth more than any bow-covered box containing yet another pair of socks, and these gifts of the spirit strengthened the two young missionaries so far from home.

❄ ❄ ❄

This cold December day had been typical. The first half of it had been spent street contacting in a commercial district near the train station. This process, dubbed *dendo* by the missionaries, consisted of approaching people as they walked past the section of street where the missionaries were positioned. This train station was one of several that supported Tokyo's massive population. Nearly eight million people passed through its doors each day.

The missionaries often felt as if they were the steel ball in a pinball machine, bouncing randomly from one person to the next. They would talk with anyone who came close to them. Sometimes they walked a few yards with their target as they tried to engage them in conversation, but most of their invitations were met with an upturned hand and a faint whisper of "*kekko desu*," signifying this individual wasn't interested. The hand represented a sort of invisible wall or barrier the elders weren't to cross. No one was belligerent; they simply weren't interested.

After a quick lunch of yakisoba noodles at a nearby *kissaten* (café), the afternoon was spent canvassing a residential section of town. Usually no one was home, and those few who were registered indifference to the message offered by the two Americans.

Tired but undeterred, the elders jumped on the train and headed back to their tiny apartment for a quick dinner before their evening appointments. It had been a crisp day, the cold temperature accentuated by the pervasive humidity, and they were grateful for the fifteen-minute ride back to their home. Despite the crowds, they welcomed these moments of rest and quiet contemplation.

"Excuse me, are you with the Mormon Church?"

The young man sitting next to Mark spoke in broken English, interrupting Mark's mental wanderings, and the young missionary shook his head to bring himself back to the present.

"Yes," he replied, hiding his surprise. "I am Elder Tanner, and," he pointed to his companion, "this is Elder Bentley."

"I am Nobuo Takahashi. I am grateful to make your acquaintance."

This was new territory for Mark, and he quickly asked a series of questions without giving his new friend a chance to answer any of them. "How do you know about the Mormon Church? How do you know English? Have you talked with missionaries before?"

A lot of the missionaries' work in Japan, at least initially, was teaching the basics of Christianity. Hence Mark's surprise when Nobuo replied, "I know a little about your church. I have read some of your Book of Mormon. Do you ever talk with people about your beliefs?"

"Uh . . . yes," stammered Mark, barely able to believe this was happening. He'd heard stories of encounters like this, but his experiences over the past year hadn't prepared him to expect one. He was so surprised that he just gazed at Nobuo, a silly grin spreading across his face.

Thankfully, Mark's companion had the presence of mind to schedule a time to meet with Nobuo. As the train approached their stop, the three men quickly shared contact information and set an appointment for the following evening.

6

THE GIFT

The next evening, Nobuo introduced the two American missionaries to his wife, Akiko, and their
two small boys, ages five and seven. The
elders bowed to her in acknowledgment
and then enthusiastically shook the boys'
hands.

The boys giggled, then laughed harder

when the Americans spoke Japanese. In turn, the boys threw every English word they knew at these strange-looking new friends. After a total of perhaps three words, the little boys exhausted their linguistic prowess. Following a few other pleasantries, the group began their discussion.

Mark and his companion learned that Nobuo had met a couple of missionaries several years earlier, when he was much younger. His family had been through the series of missionary lessons and had come close to joining the Church, but the pull of tradition had been too strong. Eventually his parents had distanced themselves from the elders, ultimately losing all contact, yet young Nobuo had felt something he'd never forgotten. When he and his wife began discussing the need to find a new direction for their family, he remembered this early experience and decided to seek out the Church again. The problem was he didn't know where to start. Just a few weeks later, he'd happened upon the missionaries on the train.

With quiet eagerness, Elder Tanner and Elder Bentley began the first lesson. Both Nobuo and Akiko readily asked questions and seemed comfortable with the answers they received, and at the end of the lesson, they willingly accepted the challenge to prayerfully read the Book of Mormon and to see the missionaries again the following evening.

The second discussion progressed much like the first. As it was concluding, Mark said, "Nobuo, Akiko, we have experienced feelings of peace with you as we have talked. This is the Holy Ghost testifying that these things are true. We have all felt this." Mark was treading on ground he had never before covered, but he felt assured and confident and was determined to be bold.

"Yes," Nobuo responded. "We have felt good about what you have taught us."

Akiko nodded her head in confirmation.

"We just read in the Book of Mormon about how Jesus was baptized to fulfill all righteousness and to be obedient to His Father in every way," Mark continued. "Will you, Nobuo and Akiko, follow the example of Jesus and be baptized as a member of His church?"

"Of course," Nobuo said matter-of-factly.

Once again, Mark was speechless, but a smile spread over the full breadth of his face.

When Elders Tanner and Bentley left the Takahashi home that evening, they didn't exult aloud, though they felt a joy that nearly consumed them. Instead, they quietly dropped to their knees at the door to the Takahashi home. In full view of the neighborhood, they expressed their gratitude to their Heavenly Father for being able to participate in this family's conversion.

The two elders felt just for a moment as Alma must have felt. They were learning what it was like to "cry repentance" to an unbelieving people and see some of them, however few, begin to feel the power of the gospel. They were learning the beauty of the plan of salvation and how, in reality, it becomes a catalyst for bringing unspeakable joy to the lives of those it touches. In this case, the lives were those of Nobuo and his little family, but the missionaries were feeling the same impact.

Their subsequent meetings went much the same way. As each gospel principle was introduced, Nobuo and his family accepted it as if they'd known it all their lives. When a commitment was required, they readily agreed as if they couldn't envision living their lives any other way.

A baptism date was set—December 25, Christmas Day. Though Christmas wasn't a universally-celebrated holiday in Japan, those in the Church acknowledged and celebrated it as the Savior's birthday. The missionaries couldn't think of a better way to mark the sacred day than to hold a baptismal service.

On Christmas Eve, the evening before the baptisms were to occur, Mark and his companion met with Nobuo and Akiko to conduct their final interviews, prepare the recommend, and review the last details of the service. They had paperwork to fill out, a customary procedure, but Nobuo's and Akiko's quiet, simple testimonies touched the elders and made completing these final details spiritually fulfilling and deeply joyful.

The interview complete, the elders sat silently contemplating the strangely solemn conclusion to a routine interview, and then Mark broke the silence in a subdued tone.

"Nobuo, I have a question that won't leave my mind. Somehow, it's important." He paused, then asked, "Why were you so prepared for this moment?"

"Pardon me?"

"You must know that we spend many hours every day trying to get people to see the simple truths you have embraced. No one seems to care. No one seems to have even the slightest desire to listen. Why did you instantly grasp and accept what we were teaching?"

Nobuo smiled. "It might seem to you that we instantly accepted this message. But you need to understand. We have been thinking about this for a long time. We have been prepared over the course of many years. We didn't realize until just recently that it was this specific message we were looking for, but we were familiar with your church, at least from a distance, and have been praying for direction." He paused. "Let me show you something."

He got up and quickly moved to an adjacent room. When he returned, he was holding a familiar blue book. The cover was a bit worn and the corners frayed slightly, but the familiar image of the angel Moroni dominated the cover.

"Where did you get that?" Mark asked incredulously. He had seen this older edition at his parents' home and knew immediately what it was: a Book of Mormon—in English.

Nobuo answered, "I told you when we first started talking that my parents once had several meetings with the missionaries. I was just a boy, but I distinctly remember the feeling I had when they were here. I remember one of the missionaries was short and kind of plump. The other was very tall and thin. They seemed an unlikely pair, but they also carried a quiet confidence that I have never forgotten. They gave my parents this book," he went on. "When I was older, I asked to have it. I read from it often when I was first learning English, and I have continued to read from it off and on for the last several years. What has been most stirring to me is what is inside the cover," Nobuo explained. "The message there has always

spoken to me insistently. I have read it many times, and I have often wished I could have the same conviction. I have finally learned that I can. This is a great gift to me."

Mark took the book gingerly in hand, feeling the reverence Nobuo's attitude conveyed. He opened the cover and saw a bold message, written in a heavy, rustic hand. As he began to read, he suddenly heard a voice from the past. With its endearing foreign accent, it clearly echoed a distant fatherland. He heard the *w*'s pronounced like *v*'s, the *th*'s like *d*'s, the *j*'s like *y*'s, and the uvular *r*'s. The testimony was in English, but Mark's mind and memory heard:

> I give you dis buch through my son. He iss a missionary. I hope you vill read dis buch. Iss da vord of Gott. From dis buch, I learn of my Savior, Jesus Christus, und He iss my Redeemer. Ven you read dis buch, I hope you vill pray about it, und you vill love my Savior as I do. Dis buch iss true.

The young missionary would never be able to adequately explain the sensation that pulsed through him. The letters of the note swam away in the flood of tears that dimmed his vision. He brushed them away, and the name of the author appeared below the note. Written in bold, painstakingly-formed letters, it leaped at him: Wilhelm Krause. Old Bill.

Gratitude overwhelmed the young missionary who had walked with the author of the brief note, whose son, many years earlier, had taught Nobuo's family. The tall frame Mark's youthful strength had steadied and supported seemed almost present to him, and the shame he had come to feel at his initial reluctance to respond to the assignment dissolved, washed away in his gratitude.

The Christmas spirit reached inside him as it never had before, even though he was far from home and Japan could never offer what ribbons, bows, packages—and yes, even lightbulbs strung along self-tangling wires—could. He sensed a depth of "Christmas Spirit" beyond anything even Charles Dickens could have envisioned. It was the season of giving, but Mark felt it as one who had received far more than he had given.

He remembered his plea to God to help him understand why this once-sturdy man clung to a much-reduced life, and his entire being was suddenly a prayer of gratitude.

"I thank thee, Father, for this Christmas gift."

ABOUT
the AUTHOR

A native of Utah's Wasatch Front, Shawn D. Moon has traveled the globe mostly for his professional career, but occasionally he travels simply to satisfy the urge to see beyond the present moment and local scenery. Accompanying him to many of these far-flung places is Michele, Shawn's wife, whom he met in the second grade. Sometime between recess and high school graduation, they fell in love, and following Shawn's service in the Pennsylvania Philadelphia Mission but before graduation from Brigham Young University, they married. After a few moves, including time in Washington, DC, they eventually settled in Lindon, Utah, with their four children. Shawn is the author of the book *On Your Own: A Young Adults' Guide to Making Smart Decisions*.

0 26575 10896 5